The Amazing Adventures of Abby McQuade

THE MORNING PEOPLE

Evan Jacobs

The Amazing Adventures of Abby McQuade

SADDLEBACK
EDUCATIONAL PUBLISHING
www.sdlback.com

ISBN-13: 978-1-68021-472-7
eBook: 978-1-63078-826-1

Printed in Malaysia

23 22 21 20 19   1 2 3 4 5

Largo Bay

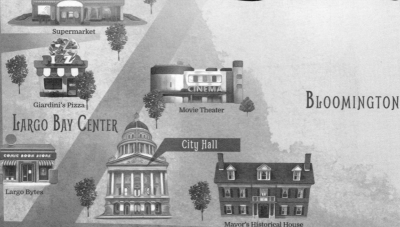

Supermarket

Giardini's Pizza

Largo Bay Center

COMIC BOOK STORE

Largo Bytes

CINEMA

Movie Theater

BLOOMINGTON

City Hall

Mayor's Historical House

GATO VILLA

Adventure Begins

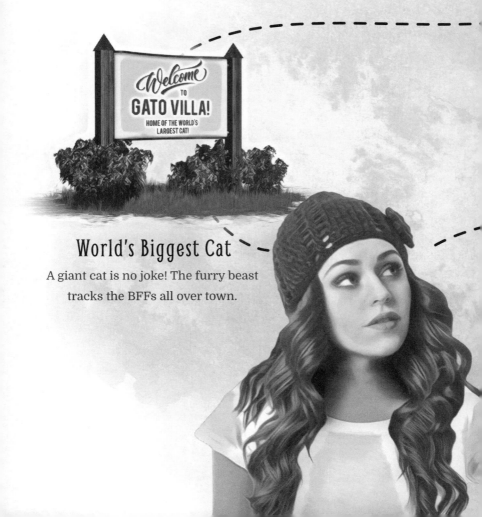

Welcome TO **GATO VILLA!** HOME OF THE WORLD'S LARGEST CAT!

World's Biggest Cat

A giant cat is no joke! The furry beast tracks the BFFs all over town.

Midnight Ride

Abby and Clara sneak out of the house.
They hop on a bus to Gato Villa.

Disco Bus

It's been real. The girls take another bus.
This is one crazy ride.

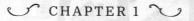

CHAPTER 1

The Sleepover

Abby was in Clara's bedroom. She was sleeping over. Sleepovers were a regular thing. Sometimes the girls would sleep in the living room. There were no rules. Usually they would watch movies till dawn. Eating junk food was a must.

They had just finished watching a movie. *The Dancing Corpse* was a horror flick. It was about a dead woman. The woman had entered a break-dancing contest. Unfortunately she died before the competition. Then she'd risen from the dead. The undead woman danced and won!

"That was so funny!" Abby laughed.

"Totally," Clara said. "Such cool break dancing."

Clara tried to do an arm wave. Abby tried popping and locking. They swung their arms wildly. The two giggled.

"That guy's head fell off," Clara said.

Abby ran her hands through her red hair. "Yeah," she said. "His head went like this." She pushed her head back with her hands. Then she fell backward with a cackle.

"Shhh!" Clara said. She muffled her giggles. "My parents are sleeping."

Abby loved movies and books. Her dad enjoyed films too. He liked ones from the 1930s and 1940s. That was why Abby had seen so many of them.

Abby's mom was a math wiz. What was cool about that? Abby didn't understand it. She was close to her folks, though. Adults were nerds sometimes.

"What should we watch next?" Abby asked.

She got up and looked through some DVDs. "What haven't we seen a million times?"

"It's almost two in the morning."

"I'm not tired." Abby turned to her friend. "Looks like you're buying doughnuts tomorrow. Again."

The girls had a game. The first person to fall asleep lost. That person had to buy doughnuts the next day.

Abby had never had to buy them.

"I'm not tired either," Clara said. She stood up. Then she jogged in place. "Look at me! I can go all night."

Abby laughed. She sorted through the movies. An idea came to her. "You want to go out?" she asked. "Let's see what the nightlife is like."

The girls lived in Largo Bay. It was an old beach town. There were homes right on the beach. Behind those were schools and more houses. Largo Bay Center was the main shopping center. There were smaller strip malls too.

Abby and Clara went to the middle school. They were eighth graders. Clara was a star swimmer. She belonged to a private swim club. Her life was very scheduled. Abby was not athletic. But she loved adventures. Weird things always seemed to happen around her.

Next to Largo Bay were two cities. One was Gato Villa. The other was Bloomington. Those places were strange. The girls thought the people there were odd. They didn't go there.

"Nightlife? Are you for real?" Clara asked, laughing. Their hometown was not a happening place. "It's late, Abby."

"So?" Abby said, smiling. "We've been out late before."

-ᛉ-

Clara smacked her forehead. *Here we go again*, her face said. The girls moved slowly down the hall. The TV was on in Clara's parents' bedroom. Her dad snored loudly.

Abby started to giggle. "He sounds like a wood chipper," she whispered.

Clara whipped around. "Shhh!"

They tiptoed down the stairs. At each step they stopped. Nobody woke up.

Thankfully some lights were on. It was easy to find their way.

"The front door, right?" Abby asked.

Clara nodded. "Yeah. It's easier. The garage is a hot mess." She reached the last step and kept moving. "Yikes!" she gasped.

Abby held her breath. Clara had stepped on a Roomba. It was a robot vacuum. At night it cleaned the floors.

She hadn't been ready for the robot. It had spun her around. Clara lost her balance. For sure her parents would wake up. Abby lunged. She grabbed her friend's arm.

The girls made eye contact.

Slowly Abby pulled her friend back to the last step. The pair tried not to giggle. They took deep breaths.

The Roomba moved into the living room. The girls crept into the front hall. Clara gently turned the deadbolt. She started to pull open the door.

Thump-thump! Thump-thump! Thump-thump!

What was that? It was Otis! He was the family's brown Labrador. The dog licked Abby's arm with his slobbery tongue. Then he nuzzled Clara.

"We can't go," Clara said. She tried to move the big dog. "He's going to bark. Open doors freak him out. If he thinks we're leaving, he will woof!"

Abby reached into the pocket of her hoodie. Inside was some popcorn. She gave a handful to Otis. He started to eat. She put more on the floor. "Okay," she whispered. "That should keep him busy."

Clara kept her eye on the dog. Then she slowly opened the door. Both girls quickly slipped outside. Otis kept eating happily.

Freedom! They had made it.

CHAPTER 2

The Escape

You had popcorn in your pocket. Why?" Clara asked. "That's gross."

"It's good to be prepared," Abby joked. "I thought I'd want a snack."

"Were there any kernels? I don't want Otis to choke."

"No," Abby said. "No kernels. I looked first."

The girls walked past Largo Bay Center. There was a big supermarket. The strip mall also had smaller shops. There was a game store. It was called Largo Bytes. The store resold video games and comic books.

Abby and Clara stared at the shops. The lights were either off or dimmed. There were no cars in the parking lot.

"This place is boring," Abby said. "What a snooze."

"Yeah," Clara said. "And it took work to leave the house."

There was a small breeze. Nothing much was happening.

"How can this town have no nightlife?" Abby asked. She looked across the street. There were some restaurants. Their lights were off too.

"There aren't any cars on the road," Clara said.

Then a lone car drove by. It went under the speed limit.

"What do you want to do?" Abby asked.

"What *can* we do? Let's go back home."

"That's kind of a letdown, Clara."

They stared at each other.

Suddenly they heard a loud squealing sound. Abby and Clara both jumped. There was a shiny silver bus. "Gato Villa," its sign read.

The bus stopped. Its doors swung open.

The driver was old. Bushy silver hair grew on each side of his head. He had a bald spot on top. His uniform was a gray jumpsuit.

There were people on the bus. The windows were foggy. Why would they be like that? It was strange. The heater wasn't needed. It wasn't cold outside.

"You two ladies coming aboard?" The driver smiled.

The girls looked around.

"Us?" Abby asked.

The driver laughed. "I don't see anyone else," he said.

"Did you bring money?" Abby asked Clara.

"No," Clara said. "Did you?"

Abby shook her head.

"It's okay," the driver said. "You girls are

in luck. Rides are free from here to Gato Villa. It's from two to five o'clock. This is the morning bus. Final stop is Gato Villa. Then it returns to Largo Bay."

"Really?" Abby asked. "The bus is free?"

"That's what I just said," the old man said. "I can say it again. Do you want me to repeat myself?"

"Let's get on," Abby said. She started up the steps.

Clara grabbed her arm. "Are you sure we can get home?" she asked the driver. "For free?"

"Got cotton in your ears? That's the deal," the driver said. "You must be back on the bus by five. Hop on."

"Come on!" Abby took Clara's hand. "Gato Villa, here we come."

CHAPTER 3

Bus Ride

There weren't many people on the bus. The girls chose a seat close to the front.

"How cool is this?" Abby asked. "We got a free ride. Did you know about this bus? Nobody told me. What an adventure!"

"Nope," Clara said. "I didn't have a clue. Um … why aren't we moving?"

At that point the old driver stood up. He grabbed a lunch box and a thermos. Then he stepped off the bus.

"What?" Abby and Clara both said.

Before they could say more, the doors closed. Then the bus started to move. There was no driver.

"Abby?" Clara started. "What is going on?"

"That is a very good question."

Abby looked at the people. None of the passengers seemed fazed. Nobody looked scared. Still, the bus was moving without a driver.

It sped up. The bus went faster. Then it slowed down at a yellow light. The light turned red. The bus stopped. It started to move when the light turned green. No traffic rules were broken.

Not having a driver was uncomfortable. The ride was smooth, though. The girls settled in.

"I didn't know there were self-driving buses," Abby said.

"Maybe they come out when it's late."

"That makes sense," Abby replied. "Fewer cars on the road."

The girls sat quietly. They enjoyed the view. The free ride was pleasant. Mellow was just how Clara liked it. Abby's adventures tended to be stressful.

"Oh yeah!" a voice called. It was the man across from them. "Now it's time to eat!"

The man wore a green shirt and blue pants. He picked up a green backpack. Then he took out a box. It was a frozen dinner.

Abby looked at him. The dinner was one of her favorites. It had fried chicken. There was also corn and mashed potatoes.

"Does the bus have an oven?" Clara asked. She looked around. "How is he going to cook that?"

The man opened the meal box. He took out the tray. Next he pulled off the plastic wrap.

"I don't see a microwave," Clara said. She was still looking around. "It doesn't look heated. I can't see any steam."

"Um, no," Abby said. "I don't think he's going to heat it."

"What?" Clara gaped.

Abby was right.

The man picked up some frozen chicken. Then he started to lick it. He took out a fork. It was a good tool to use. He chipped away at the vegetables.

"That is so gross," Clara whispered. She quickly looked away.

"Maybe he likes it that way," Abby said. She couldn't help but smile. Clara was easily grossed out.

The girls looked behind them. What did other people think? Nobody blinked.

There was a woman on the bus. Next to her was a black Doberman pinscher. The dog stared straight ahead. It didn't move and barely blinked.

The woman held up her phone.

Is she taking a selfie? Abby thought. *That dog won't pose for her. This is hilarious.*

"Do you like it, Daddy?" the woman asked.

Hmm, Abby thought. *That's an unusual name for a dog.*

The lady wrapped her arms around the dog. It didn't move. The animal stared straight ahead. The woman didn't give up. "Hey, Daddy," she said. "Do you like this *Barney* video? Have I been good?"

Abby couldn't believe it. She stared. Clara stared too. It was rude. The girls had good manners. But something was off about this bus.

"Is she showing her dog a *Barney* video?" Clara asked. "I stopped watching those when I was three."

"Me too," Abby said. "And 'Daddy' isn't the dog's name. It's not like Rover or Max. I think she thinks the dog *is* her dad."

The girls checked out the woman again.

The lady petted the dog's head. Then her attention moved to the video. "I love *Barney*," she said. "It's the best show."

The dog didn't budge. It was like the phone wasn't there.

"Have you done your holiday shopping?" the woman asked. "I've been a good girl. A doll would be nice. Also a new bike. I want some video games too."

Abby and Clara looked at each other.

"Let's stop staring," Abby said. "It's rude."

"Agreed," Clara said.

They both faced forward.

"See? She really thinks the dog is her dad," Abby said.

Clara shrugged.

Ding! Ding!

"Gato Villa," an electronic voice said. "Last stop."

Soon the bus pulled over. Then it stopped. Abby and Clara stood up. They moved to the doors.

The man eating his dinner smiled at them. He took a bite of his frozen food.

Abby and Clara smiled too.

The woman with the dog waved.

The girls waved back.

Everyone moved toward the front. It was time to get off the bus.

These people were different. But so what? Abby and Clara were too—sometimes. That was not an excuse to be rude or unkind.

CHAPTER 4

Gato Villa

Abby and Clara walked along a strip mall. Shops were closed. "For Rent" signs were in the windows. The stores had gone out of business.

The girls had always lived in Largo Bay. They had never been to Gato Villa. It was the same with Bloomington. People there were different. They had unusual habits and manners.

It was as if everyone lived on separate planets. There was no reason to go. Well, there was one reason. You had to drive through those towns. Otherwise you'd never go anywhere.

"Can you believe that man? He was

eating frozen food." Clara shivered. Her face scrunched up. "Just thinking about it makes me sick."

"Maybe he was hungry," Abby said. "I've eaten some gross stuff. Especially when I've been hungry."

"But not frozen chicken," Clara snapped. "And what was up with that pet owner?"

"She thinks the dog is her dad," Abby said. "Maybe her dad died. Reincarnation is possible …" Abby's voice trailed off.

Clara shot her friend a look. Abby shrugged.

"You know what?" Clara said. "I'm an accepting person. Never have I seen anything like that."

"Well, we don't ride the bus much. Maybe it wouldn't look weird if we did."

Abby thought about it. Was that what it was like? Bus rides were sweet! Maybe this ride had opened up a new world. This was an entirely different nightlife.

The girls came up to a big sign. It said, "Welcome to Gato Villa! Home of the World's Largest Cat!"

Abby took out her phone. "Stand in front of the sign, Clara," she said.

"No way," Clara said. "I don't want anyone to know I was here."

"Gosh, you don't sound very accepting. Snobbish much?"

"Fine." Clara stood in front of the sign. She folded her arms.

Abby snapped the picture. She thought it looked good.

"Are you going to post it?" Clara asked.

"Should I?" Abby hadn't thought about it. Posting it on social media would be cool.

"Not the best plan," Clara said. "Do you want our parents to know? We did sneak out."

"Good point." Abby put her phone away.

They continued to walk. Eventually they saw a mobile home park. The homes looked old. A strong wind would blow them all away.

"Okay," Clara finally said. "I think I'm good with Gato Villa."

"What do you mean? We just got here."

"Yeah. There's nothing to do here."

"Duh. It's almost three in the morning."

"Don't I know it," Clara said. "Now I'm starting to get sleepy."

"We just got off the bus." Abby turned and pointed. "You can see the back of Largo Bay Center. Home isn't too far away. We've never been here."

"There's a reason for that!" Clara fumed.

"Let's explore a little more. Please?"

"All right," Clara said. "But all it takes is one more weird thing. Then I'm calling it. We're going home. Okay?"

"Deal."

Abby put her arm through Clara's. The pair moved on.

Suddenly a large black SUV screeched to

the curb. "Gato Villa Devils" was printed on the side. The letters were white. The words really popped.

People got out of the SUV. They all wore black. Some wore T-shirts and jeans. Others wore tank tops and jeans. There was a mix of girls and boys. Two girls stepped forward. One had black hair. The other had blonde hair.

A white van pulled up next. It parked in front of the SUV.

The people in the van stepped out. The girls wore skirts. The boys wore khakis. Everyone wore jean jackets. "Bloomington Crazies" was printed on the back. Two girls moved ahead. One had a shaved head. The other was a brunette.

The boys and girls looked like high school students.

The Devils in black moved to the Crazies in jackets.

"You guys stole our friend's cell phone!" a Devil said. She had black hair.

"You guys slashed the tires on our van!" a Crazy said. Her head was shaved.

Most girls don't look good bald, Abby thought. *Not this chick. She looks cool.*

"Why are you in Gato Villa?" the blonde girl snapped. "You aren't welcome here." For sure she was the leader's sidekick. The black-haired Devil was in charge, 100 percent.

"We'll go where we want!" the brunette girl yelled. She was the Crazies' second in command, for sure.

The two groups inched closer to each other. Other people gathered.

"Oh my gosh!" Clara cried. "They're going to fight."

Everybody yelled. The two groups pushed and shoved. A full-scale riot was about to break out.

"Hey!" Abby yelled. "You guys!"

Suddenly there was silence. All eyes were on Abby McQuade.

"What?" the leaders from both groups snapped. The black-haired girl stared at Abby. The bald girl snorted.

"Stop! You can't fight." Abby was thinking fast. She had stopped fights before. But this was a gang fight. It was different.

"Why can't we?" the Devils' leader asked.

"Yeah," the Crazies' leader said. "Isn't it past your bedtime, little girl?"

"Yes, it is," Abby said with a smile. "It's past all of our bedtimes. Why don't we all go home? Let's get a good night's sleep. We'll wake up fresh. Nobody will want to fight."

"Oh?" the blonde said. "I *want* to fight someone." She smirked.

"Me too," the brunette said.

Then they both moved toward Abby. The girls pounded their fists.

CHAPTER 5

The Cat

You!" the gang girls said at the same time.

"Me?" Abby cried. She backed into Clara. They both moved away from the gangs.

The gangbangers blocked them. The crowd around them cheered.

"But—" Abby started.

"But what?" the Devils' leader asked. She grabbed Abby's hoodie.

The crowd cheered louder.

"Fighting is *so* lame!" Abby yelled.

"Are you calling us lame?" The Crazies' leader also grabbed Abby's hoodie.

"Why do you want to fight?" Abby asked.

"It's something to do," the Devils' leader said. "All right?"

"True," Abby said. "But you'll get in big trouble."

The fighters stared at the girls. Then they started to cackle. The crowd laughed too. Everybody was cracking up—except for Clara.

"Where are you from?" a Crazy asked.

"Largo Bay," Abby said softly.

"Where? Speak up!" a Devil yelled.

"Largo Bay."

The gangbangers looked at each other. Then their attention turned back to Abby.

"The Gato Villa Devils hate that town!" the blonde said.

"The Bloomington Crazies hate it even more!" the brunette snapped.

"Why?" Abby asked. "It's just a quiet town. Nobody does anything. We're sandwiched between your two cities. Nothing happens there."

"It's not the town," the Crazies' leader said. "It's the people there. They are so rude."

"People act like they're the best. Everyone has attitude."

"No," Abby said. "We don't."

"Abby," Clara said nervously. "Maybe you should agree with them."

"But they're wrong, Clara."

"Ooh," the Crazies' leader said. "Now she's telling us we're dumb."

"You know what?" the Devils' leader asked. "She needs to say sorry."

"Nah. That would be too easy," the Crazies' leader said. "Let's rearrange her face."

The crowd loved those words. "Fight! Fight! Fight!" they chanted.

The Devils' leader pulled her arm back. "Sorry, kid," she said. "But you've got a big mouth."

The other leader made a fist.

Abby closed her eyes. She had never been beaten up. This was her first fight.

The crowd quieted down. They waited for the punch.

Meow! Meow! Meow!

Abby slowly opened her eyes.

The gang leaders stopped. Their fists were frozen.

Everyone looked around.

Meow! Meow! Meow!

There it was again!

"It's the *gato!*" a man in the crowd yelled. "Run! Run!"

People freaked out. Everyone scattered.

The gangs ran to their cars. Tires screeched as they drove away.

"What's going on?" Clara asked.

Meow! Meow! Meow!

"That sounds fake," Abby said. "At least it got me out of a beating."

Then the girls heard a stomping sound.

"Ab-by," Clara said anxiously. "What was that?"

They turned. The streets were empty. There were no cars. A few people hid.

Abby looked in the direction of the sound. She poked Clara's ribs. "Look up," she mouthed.

No way! It was unbelievable. The girls blinked. Their eyes focused. There it was. No wonder the town was called Gato Villa.

The black cat was one street over. It was 25 feet tall!

The animal was at least three buses high. It had big black eyes. Gray whiskers were 10 feet long. Sharp white teeth sparkled in its mouth.

"Abby," Clara said. "Look out! It's coming this way."

The cat started to run. Its eyes were fixed on the girls.

Everybody hiding moved. There were muffled screams.

Abby grabbed her friend's hand. They ran.

Clara couldn't take her eyes off the beast. "That is a *Guinness World Record* cat!" she cried.

"Snap out of it!" Abby called. "Focus on running."

The girls ran by good hiding spots. People had already taken them. Then they went down a short street. It was lined with cul-de-sacs.

No way were they stopping. The giant cat was scary. Now was not the time to check a map. They were stuck, though. Every street was a dead end. Fewer people were out.

Soon the girls noticed they were alone. The streets were deserted. The cat had disappeared.

That was the good news. The bad news was they were lost. They were in a neighborhood.

There were many homes and no stores. Where in Gato Villa were they?

"What now?" Clara asked. "I always listen to you. 'Let's go out,' you said. 'It will be fun,' you said. This is not fun."

Meow! Meow! Meow!

No! It was that darn cat.

CHAPTER 6

Car Chase

"We keep moving," Abby said. "Come on!"

"I thought we'd lost it," Clara said. "I am so tired. You would think I'd be in shape. All that swimming and training I do. But I'm pooped running from this cat."

"Why is it following us?" Abby cried.

The cat howled. It sounded farther away.

The girls looked up. There it was again. It was taller than the houses. At least it wasn't too close.

"It's three streets over," Clara said. "What is it looking for?"

"I don't know. Let's keep moving." Abby took out her phone.

"What are you doing?"

The girls jogged slowly down a street. Hopefully this one wasn't a dead end. Somebody had to help them get out of this town.

"I need to take a picture. Or do you think a video is better?"

"What? I think living is better! That cat is huge. It could swallow us both in one gulp."

Click.

Abby took a picture. She checked it. It was too dark. Nobody would recognize the image.

Clack-clack! Clack-clack! Clack-clack!

It was a different sound. The girls stopped.

"Did you hear something?" Abby asked.

"I know *I* heard it," Clara grumbled. "You were busy taking pictures."

"Oh snap."

It was a clacking sound. The sound got louder.

Three skateboards headed their way. There were no skaters!

One was in the front. Two were behind the first. Those two were side by side. The three formed a triangle. The boards rumbled along the road. They were going at a reasonable speed.

Abby lifted up her phone. This was too good. Nobody would believe her. She needed proof.

Click.

She checked it. The image was blurry. The boards were black. They blended into the street.

"That was sick!" she said. She tried to snap another picture. It was too late. The skateboards were gone. They had made a right turn. "Let's follow them."

"No freakin' way!" Clara said.

Tick-tick-tick! Tick-tick-tick! Tick-tick-tick!

It was yet another sound. The girls' eyes followed their ears. Four riderless bicycles went by. The bikes went two by two.

Click.

Abby snapped another picture. The bikes moved faster than the skateboards. The image was blurry again. Nobody was going to believe this. Abby was frustrated.

"Gato Villa is weird," Clara said. "Where are we going? I feel like we're walking in circles. This doesn't feel like Mazey Pines, though."

"Mazey Pines is dope," Abby said. It was a neighborhood in Largo Bay. Pine trees appeared. They formed a maze. It only happened at certain times. People got stuck there. "But it's crazy in a cool way. This place is odd. Maybe because it's so late. It could be normal during the day."

"Uh-huh," Clara said doubtfully. "Maybe."

"We will have to come back again," Abby said. "Then we'll know for sure."

"*Ha-ha-ha*," Clara laughed. "No thanks." She rolled her eyes.

Abby laughed too. Clara was always over it before she was. Adventures were awesome.

"Are we walking in the right direction? Will we end up near home? My feet hurt."

"I think so," Abby replied. "It feels like we're walking toward the ocean. I feel the breeze."

"Oh, duh! Let's use the GPS on our phones," Clara said. "Or a map app. We can look for bus stops too."

"Yes! Smart move. Why didn't I think of that?" Abby unlocked her phone again. She started to open the app.

Vroom! Vroom! Vroom!

An engine revved in the distance. There was a car at the far end of the street. It was too dark to get a good look. The headlights were off.

Abby and Clara stopped moving. This was not the time to turn around. They would be farther from home.

"We have to go back," Abby said. "Just for now. I know it's the wrong way."

"This is getting old."

They about-faced. There was yet another car. It revved its engine too. Now the girls were trapped.

The car in front turned on its lights. Then the car behind did the same. Both came toward them. They were in the middle.

"Ab-by," Clara said with fear. "I don't have a good feeling. They're not going to offer us a ride home."

Soon both cars were 10 feet away. The girls

could see who was in each. Ugh. Their hearts sank.

In one car were the Gato Villa Devils. The Bloomington Crazies were in the other one.

The black-haired girl got out of one car. Abby remembered she was the Devils' leader. Her blonde sidekick followed.

Then the other car's door opened. The girl with the shaved head got out. The Crazies' leader looked mad. The brunette trailed her.

"Well, well, well," the Devils' leader said, smirking. "If it isn't the Largo Bay Babies."

"Now, where were we?" the Crazies' leader asked. "That darn cat rudely interrupted us."

Abby looked at her friend. She took her hand. Then she ran, yanking Clara with her. The four gangbangers sprinted after them.

Tires screeched. Engines roared. The others followed by car.

Abby and Clara had to escape. They raced

across people's lawns. Where was the main street?

"These are all dead ends!" Clara cried.

Abby ignored her. They had to keep going. There had to be a way out.

"You can run," the Devils' leader called. "But you can't hide."

The cars sounded louder now. They were close. It wouldn't be long.

Suddenly the giant black cat stepped out. Abby and Clara ran under its big hairy legs. They ducked and missed its swatting tail. The two kept running.

Behind them, the cat hissed. The cars braked hard. Abby thought the girls chasing them had stopped too. Nobody wanted to tangle with the cat.

Now Abby and Clara were on the main road. Somehow they'd made it. There was a bus at the corner. Its doors were open.

A man stepped off. He wore a pink tutu.

In his hands were some plates. He started to juggle. Up and down went the plates. Then they went higher and higher.

Normally this would be epic. The girls just rolled their eyes. This was one strange night. Quickly they jumped onto the bus. Safe!

Neither girl had read the sign. The bus was headed to Bloomington.

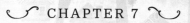

CHAPTER 7

Blast Off

Abby and Clara took a seat. Like before, they sat in the front. This time they didn't have a choice. The bus was full.

This bus had a driver. The girls were relieved. In fact, it was the same driver.

"The old dude is back," Abby said. "Maybe he had to take a break."

"No offense, Abby. Who cares? I want to go home. It's time to sleep."

The girls sat there, resting. Clara's nose wrinkled. So did Abby's. The bus had an aroma. It wasn't good.

Clara looked at her bestie. They both made a face. What was that smell? The two checked out the other passengers.

Everybody was eating. Some people ate sushi. Others ate pastrami sandwiches. Some were eating greasy pizza. The oil dripped onto the floor.

Above them was a disco ball.

"Maybe the food is the source," Abby said. "It smells nasty."

"How can they eat so late?" Clara asked.

The pair noticed something else. Gnats flew around. People ignored the bugs.

"Why are they still munching?" Clara asked. "Those bugs are gross. I'd feel sick."

"I guess they're hungry," Abby said. She looked out the window. Up ahead she saw Largo Bay Center.

Clara saw it too. "Pull the cord," she ordered.

Abby reached up. She yanked it. The driver would have to stop.

Nothing happened.

"Wait! Hey!" Clara said. "We passed it."

"Excuse me," Abby called. She stood up. Clara did too. Abby approached the driver.

"I pulled the cord," Abby said. "We wanted to stop at Largo Bay Center."

The driver didn't respond. He stared straight ahead.

Then the girls realized something. The driver wasn't human. It was a robot. This was not the same driver at all. The robot just looked like the old man.

"He's not real," Abby said.

Suddenly the bus went dark. The disco ball glowed. It started to spin.

"Now what?" Clara asked.

The two looked around.

Food was put away. Passengers got out of their seats. The seats folded into the floor.

"Thriller," by Michael Jackson, started to play on the speakers.

Whoa! It was a flash mob. Everybody started to dance. People's moves mirrored the music video. Their steps were perfect. The break dancing was on point.

"This is amazing!" Abby squealed.

Even Clara smiled.

The girls started to dance too. They couldn't help it. The power of "Thriller" was no joke.

The bus rumbled down the road. The robot driver did its job. The music didn't move him.

The song was at the best part. People stopped dancing. They went to overhead bins. Inside were backpacks. Each person got one. They put them on. Abby and Clara were given packs.

"Let's put them on too," Clara said.

"Okay," Abby said.

"Oh, it's heavy."

"What's this for?" Abby asked. There were cords on each backpack.

The top of the bus began to open. Then the floor moved upward. It sped up.

Whoosh!

People were shot high into the air.

"Aaahhh!" the girls screamed.

They were headed to the clouds. Everyone started to pull their cords. The bags opened. Parachutes popped out.

Abby and Clara did the same. Their parachutes snapped open too. The girls floated slowly. They could see everything. Bloomington. Largo Bay. Gato Villa. Las Cuevas. They even saw the ocean.

Normally Abby was afraid of heights. Right now she had no fear.

"Abby! What just happened?"

"Well," Abby called back. "We just had the best bus ride ever!"

Slowly the girls drifted to the ground. They landed on their feet. So did the other passengers.

"Epic!" Abby cried.

A sign was a few feet away. "Welcome to Bloomington! You'll Have a Blast!" it read.

CHAPTER 8

Bank Heist

No! No way!" Clara sobbed, stomping her feet. "I want to go home. Right now!"

"Yes, I know. Calm down. We made it," Abby said soothingly. "Let's talk about how rad that was. We just got shot out of a bus! There was a flash mob. What about the 25-foot tall monster cat?"

"That's great. Now I'm over it," Clara said flatly. "I want to get some sleep. No more cats. No more buses. I don't want to get shot into the air. Sleep! That's all I care about."

Abby wanted to say more. She looked at her friend. Talking right now would be wrong. It was almost four in the morning. Clara was fried.

The girls walked along a strip mall. Unlike Gato Villa, there were some open stores. Houses were behind the stores. Bloomington looked a lot like home.

They passed what looked like a club. There was a bright white sign. The club was called the Lynchpin. Jazz music was playing.

Abby could hear drums, a sax, and a bass guitar. "This music is cool," she said. "It's mellow."

"It's all right."

"Will would like it, I'll bet." Abby smiled. "That boy loves jazz."

Clara perked up. Will's name got her to focus. She had a crush on him. Of course he was clueless.

Will Chu was Abby and Clara's best guy friend. They had known him forever. He wanted to become a scientist. Computers and gadgets were his jam. So was music. He even played guitar.

The Lynchpin was crowded. There were tables and chairs outside. People sat there. They sipped espresso.

The men wore black sunglasses, black turtlenecks, and jeans. The women wore long black skirts and black shirts. Some people wore berets.

"Those were beatniks," Abby said as they walked past.

"Beat what?" Clara asked.

"Beatniks," Abby said. "In the 1950s and 1960s, they were big. They drank a lot of coffee. Now we'd call them hipsters. Beatniks were intellectuals. At least they thought they were. My parents told me about them."

"They sound weird."

"Weird is not bad. It's just different."

They walked on. Eventually the pair came

to a business district. The streets were quiet. Some shops were open. A bank looked closed. Abby didn't see many people.

"It's relaxing here," Abby said. "I love it."

"There's a bus stop," Clara said. She pointed up the street. There was a single bench. A sign was next to it.

"Let's see. When is the next one coming?" Abby took out her phone. Why walk over if they didn't have to? It would be pointless. A bus needed to come soon.

Suddenly three men ran out of the bank. They were dressed in black. Each man held a large bag.

Ring! Ring! Ring!

The sound got louder.

As the men ran, money flew out of the bags.

Abby picked up a bill. $100!

Clara picked up another one. Yikes! $100 again!

"Oh no!" Abby said. "Those men robbed that bank!"

Clara was speechless. She stared at the escaping thieves.

The bank's alarm kept ringing. This town was not mellow now.

Abby grabbed her friend's hand. Yet again Clara was yanked along.

"Wait! What? Where are we going, Abby?"

"Those guys stole that money. We've got to stop them."

Abby flipped on her camera. This time it would work. She was sure she could get a clear shot.

A car came up out of nowhere. It screeched to a stop. The trunk popped open. The crooks threw their bags into it.

Abby stopped running.

Clara slammed into her. "Hey!" she yelled.

"Let me take some pictures," Abby said.

The girls stood under a streetlight. The

lighting was good. Abby could get a clear shot. The thieves were busted now! It would be easy for the police to ID them.

Then somebody smacked the phone from her hand. It was the leader of the Gato Villa Devils. She'd been driving the getaway car.

"Hey, ouch!" Abby yelled. To herself she thought, *Of course she's the driver*. "Can I have my phone back?"

"Hello," the Devils' leader said, grinning. "Who do we have here? Look what the cat dragged in." She put Abby's phone into her pocket.

Abby and Clara noticed the black SUV. It was behind them. The Devils gang had arrived. There was a white van too. Uh-oh, the Bloomington Crazies had joined in.

The Crazies' leader approached. "Let one go," she said. "If she comes back, she's yours."

Abby and Clara started to run. It was too late.

"Nah," the Devils' leader said. "It's easier to grab both."

Abby and Clara were thrown into the getaway car. They were stuck. The thieves sat on either side of them.

"Shotgun!" the Crazies' leader called out. "Girl, you drive."

"I'm on it," the Devils' leader said.

Being with the crooks was bad enough. Now the gang leaders hopped into the front seat. Those girls hated their guts.

CHAPTER 9

Fight Club

Let's bounce!" the Devil said. The engine was running. She stepped on the gas. The tires squealed. The car took off.

The Crazy turned. She looked at Abby and Clara.

The bank robbers hadn't moved a muscle. Nobody spoke.

"Um," Abby said. She bit her lip. "We haven't put on our seat belts."

"No worries," the Crazy said. She made a fist. "You two have other problems."

"Yeah," the Devil said. "Normally my rival and I hate each other."

"We were supposed to fight tonight," the Crazy said.

"But then we met you two," the Devil said. "And that changed everything."

"Yeah," agreed the Crazy. "We hate Largo Bay. Fighting each other is boring. But you girls? Bring it!"

Everyone in the car laughed. Abby and Clara looked glum.

"We're besties now," the Devil said. "You want to know why? Let's say we had fought. Then this car would have been late. Our brothers would have been busted. Thank you."

"You're thanking us? You won't beat us up?" Clara asked.

"Not a chance," the Crazy said.

"Wait a minute," Abby said. "Brothers? Like your *real* brothers?"

The gang girls nodded.

"Let me get this straight," Abby said. "The

boys are friends. But you girls are enemies."

"We *were* enemies," the Devil said. "Until we met you."

Everyone in the car laughed again. Neither Abby nor Clara found it funny.

There was a large warehouse ahead. The car pulled up to the curb. Other cars were parked in front.

"Get out!" the gang girls ordered.

Abby and Clara got out of the car. The Devils' leader pushed Abby into the building. The Crazies' leader pushed Clara along too.

Inside, the warehouse was packed. There were beatniks, surfers, and punk rockers. The gangbangers were there as well.

The crowd cheered. The noise was deafening.

In the center was a boxing ring. It was roped off. Abby and Clara were led in.

A bank robber pushed Abby into the ring. He grabbed some boxing gloves. She had to put them on. Then he laced them. The guy stepped aside.

The Devils' leader got into the ring. The Crazies' leader stood behind her. They both wore boxing gloves.

"Hold it," Abby said. "I can't fight you."

"You don't have a choice," the Devil said. "Girl, you're first. Then it's your friend's turn."

"What?" Clara screamed.

The Crazy smiled. She pounded her gloves together.

A bell sounded.

The Devil charged toward Abby. She dodged the punch.

The crowd cheered. "Hit her! Hit her!" they called.

"Wait a minute!" Abby yelled. "This is dumb. I can't fight."

"Too late! Looks like you already are," the Devil said.

"Are we boxing?" Abby asked. "Marquis of Queensbury rules? I learned that online. Or is this MMA?"

"I'm going to enjoy shutting you up!" The Devil threw a punch.

Abby ducked. She stepped back.

The gang girl moved forward. She threw right hooks. Left hooks. Uppercuts. Body shots.

Abby ducked again. She blocked. At one point she danced. Her opponent was fast.

"Is that all you got?" the Devil yelled. "You're always talking. Do something!"

"I told you!" Abby screamed. "I don't want to fight you."

"Girl, it's too late."

The two moved around the ring a few times. Nobody landed a hit.

The crowd hollered and cheered. "Fight! Fight! Fight!" they called.

Clara covered her eyes.

Abby was getting tired. Any minute she would get hit. Her plan was not working.

"Hit her!" Clara finally screamed.

"Yeah! Do it!" the Devil teased. "Or are you chicken?"

Abby took a step back.

The other girl lunged ahead.

This was it. Abby closed her eyes. She drew her right arm back. Then she thrust it forward.

Smack!

It was a direct hit. The crowd gasped.

The Devil stopped moving.

There was total silence. Nobody said a word.

"You hit me," the girl finally cried. She sounded shocked.

"You told me to."

Tears welled up in the girl's eyes. She put her gloved hand on her cheek. "You weren't really supposed to."

"Huh?" Abby said. "I'm so sorry. I don't ever fight. Fighting is wrong. I'm not a violent person. Archery is cool. So is—"

"Stop!" The Devil held up her glove. "You talk too much. Just hush. You got some pop in those fists. I guess kids from Largo Bay aren't bad. Maybe you do have a heart. There's no need to fight. Go home, girlfriend. I'm sorry I misjudged you. Your town is okay."

Flo Rida's "Good Feeling" started to play. People danced out.

Soon only Abby and Clara were left.

"Um, Abby?" Clara asked. "What just happened?"

CHAPTER 10

Doughnut Dream

Abby and Clara started to walk. They headed home.

"I don't get it. What was the point?" Clara asked. "The Devil wanted to fight. You hit her. She begged you to do it. Then she stopped the fight. Weird."

"Maybe we were being schooled," Abby said.

A clock on the street said it was 5:03 a.m. There were no cars on the road. The free buses had stopped running. Abby and Clara had no money.

Bloomington was about five miles from home.

"How?" Clara asked. "What were we supposed to learn?"

"We think these people are weird. They think we're stuck up. Maybe there shouldn't be any labels. People are people."

"I guess," Clara said. "But we could have talked it out. Maybe shared an ice cream."

An engine roared behind them. They both turned around.

Not again! It was the two gang leaders. The black SUV stopped next to them. The Devil was driving. The Crazy sat next to her.

"Do you need a ride?" the driver asked.

"No," Clara said. "Thanks but we're fine."

Abby gave her friend a look. "Yes," she said. She smiled at the leaders. "We'd love one."

Clara rolled her eyes. Then she sighed. "Thank you," she said as she climbed in.

"Yeah," Abby agreed. "This is nice of you."

"Uh-huh," the Devil said. She patted

the Crazy's shoulder. "If Baldy and I can be friends, we can too."

"I agree. I'm Abby, by the way."

"I'm Clara."

"I'm Malena," the Devil said.

"I'm Bernadette," the Crazy said. "But I guess Baldy works too."

They all laughed.

"Hey, guys, want a doughnut?" Bernadette asked. She held up a bag. "The Doughnut Shop" was written on it.

"Yum," Abby said. "Yes, please."

"Okay," Clara said, shrugging.

Bernadette held the bag out to them. Abby reached inside. She took out a chocolate doughnut. It had chocolate frosting. Clara got a cake doughnut. It had vanilla frosting. There were colorful sprinkles on it.

"Where did your brothers go?" Abby asked. She took a bite.

Clara elbowed her friend.

"They went back to the bank," Malena said.

"For more cash?" Abby couldn't believe it. "That's just—"

"No, you nosy girl. They're returning it. You were right. Stealing is uncool. By the way, here. I'm sorry." Malena reached into her pocket. She took out Abby's phone and handed it to her.

"Thanks for giving it back. My parents would have been mad."

The seats were comfortable. The girls ate their doughnuts in silence.

Abby looked out the window. Was it morning? It was still dark. They passed strip malls and neighborhoods. Soon they would be back at Clara's.

Abby looked at her bestie. "You don't owe me doughnuts anymore," she whispered. Her eyes felt heavy.

The game they played was a sleepover

favorite. But Clara was already asleep. Abby yawned again. She stared at the road …

-᙭-

Abby woke up. She was on the floor. Clara was lying across her bed. The girls still wore street clothes.

The sun was shining. Abby looked at her phone. 10:34 a.m.

"Clara," she called.

There was no answer.

"Clara," she said again. She sat up. "It's late morning."

"What?" Clara moaned.

"Do you remember what happened?" she asked. "We're back in your room. Did we sneak in?"

"I don't remember …" Clara's voice trailed off. She had fallen asleep again.

Abby had no memory of being dropped off. What had happened? The gang girls didn't even know the address.

-ᛗ-

A few months went by. Abby and Clara
had more sleepovers. At every one, they
would sneak out. It was always around
two o'clock.

There were no free buses. The giant cat
never appeared. The riderless skateboards
and bikes had gone. Malena and Bernadette
didn't show up either. There were no beatniks,
jazz clubs, or flash mobs. Where were all the
morning people?

One day they were at Giardini's. It served
the best pizza in Largo Bay. The place was
small. There were only a few tables. On the
walls were paintings of Italy. The owners
liked opera music. It played over a crackly
speaker.

The girls had ordered two personal pizzas.
The pies hadn't been served yet.

"Maybe we did dream it all," Clara said.

She took a sip of water. "But it felt real."

"It wasn't a dream," Abby said. "There was an order of events. Things happened in sequence. We went out at a specific time. It allowed us to see some weird stuff."

"Did we enter a parallel universe?"

"Maybe."

"Will we ever see it again?"

Abby thought about it. "I don't know," she said. "We did learn about people from those towns."

"Yeah. We learned what we already knew. Those places are strange." Clara laughed.

"Like this place isn't weird?" Abby said. "Crazy stuff has gone down right here. True or not true?"

"True, but—"

The server came out. She put the pizzas on the table. Abby had gotten pepperoni. Clara's had green peppers.

Then the server put another pizza down. Half was pepperoni. The other half had green peppers.

"Oh," Abby said. "We only ordered two."

"It's all good," the server said. "You girls get some extra."

Abby and Clara looked up. It was Malena! Her black hair had blue streaks. It was in a bun. She winked and walked away.

"Abby," Clara started. "That's—"

"I know," Abby said, cutting her off.

They watched as Malena helped other customers. Giardini's was getting busy.

"We should ask her what went down," Clara said.

"I don't know."

"What?" Clara picked up a slice. "You're the most curious girl ever. How can you say that?"

"That's not it," Abby said. "I'm thrilled to see her. Our new friend gave us more pizza."

The two girls laughed. More pizza was never a bad thing.

Maybe they would talk with Malena. Or they wouldn't. A little mystery never hurt.

Right then, having all the answers didn't seem important. Abby was happy to chill with her best friend.

The Amazing Adventures of
Abby McQuade

More Amazing Adventures with Abby

BACK TO THE PAST
978-1-68021-470-3

DAYLIGHT SAVING
978-1-68021-474-1

THE GHOSTS OF LARGO BAY
978-1-68021-466-6

THE LADY FROM THE CAVES
978-1-68021-471-0

LUCKY DOLL
978-1-68021-473-4

MAZEY PINES
978-1-68021-469-7

THE MORNING PEOPLE
978-1-68021-472-7

SCREAM NIGHT
978-1-68021-468-0

VIRUS
978-1-68021-467-3